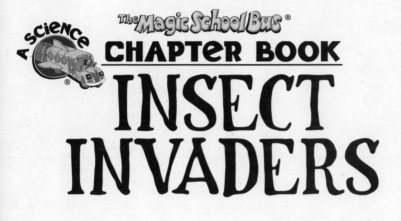

The Magic School Bus®
A science CHAPTER BOOK
INSECT INVADERS

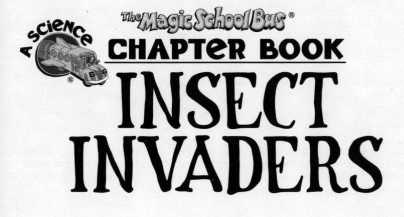

The Magic School Bus®
A Science CHAPTER BOOK
INSECT INVADERS

SCHOLASTIC INC.
New York   Toronto   London   Auckland   Sydney
Mexico City   New Delhi   Hong Kong   Buenos Aires

Written by Anne Capeci.

Illustrations by John Spiers.

Based on *The Magic School Bus* books
written by Joanna Cole and illustrated by Bruce Degen.

ISBN 0-439-31431-3

36 35 34 33 32 31 30 29   8/0

Designed by Peter Koblish

Printed in the U.S.A.   40

The author would like to thank Louis N. Sorkin, B.C.E.,
of the American Museum of Natural History's Entomology Section
for his expert advice in preparing this manuscript.

INTRODUCTION

My name is Wanda. I am one of the kids in Ms. Frizzle's class.

Maybe you have heard of Ms. Frizzle. (Sometimes we just call her the Friz.) She is a terrific teacher — but strange. One of her favorite subjects is science, and she knows *everything* about it.

She takes us on lots of field trips in the Magic School Bus. Believe me, it's not called *magic* for nothing! We never know what's going to happen when we get on that bus.

Ms. Frizzle likes to surprise us, but we

can usually tell when she is planning a special lesson. We just look at what she's wearing.

One day Ms. Frizzle showed up wearing this. As soon as I saw all those bugs, I knew we were in for a wild adventure. And when I say *wild*, I mean it! Want to hear the whole story? Here's what happened. . . .

 CHAPTER 1

"Make way for Spot and Whirly!" I said.

I carried a tissue box carefully into Ms. Frizzle's classroom. Kids were all over the place, putting away jackets and lunches and books. I was lucky to get to my desk without anyone knocking the box out of my hands.

"You gave names to your *tissues*?" Tim said, staring at the box. "That's weird."

"This *is* Ms. Frizzle's class," Carlos pointed out. "Around here, weird is normal!"

"Don't remind me," groaned Arnold.

"But those are still strange names for tissues," Keesha said.

They would be strange names for tissues, but Spot and Whirly were perfect names for my pet ladybugs! I held out the box so everyone could see.

"Cool!" said Dorothy Ann. (We usually just call her D.A.) She looked through the screen I had taped across the opening of the box. Behind it, Spot and Whirly crawled around on some leaves. "They look like tiny red balls with black spots, legs, and antennae."

"I didn't know ladybugs could be pets," Keesha said.

"Well, I'm not exactly sure how to take care of Spot and Whirly," I admitted. "I just found them in my backyard yesterday. I don't even know what they eat. I brought them in, so I could find out more about them."

"You're not the only one with bugs on

the brain, Wanda," said Tim. "Check out Ms. Frizzle's outfit."

The Friz had just walked into our classroom. Maybe I should say she *buzzed* in. With those fake antennae sticking out of her headband and pictures of dragonflies, beetles, and other bugs on her overalls, she looked a lot like an insect herself. As usual, Liz, the class lizard, was on her shoulder.

"The teachers never bugged out at my old school," said Phoebe.

But I was glad to see all those creatures. If there was anyone who could tell me how to care for Spot and Whirly, it was the Friz! I hurried over and showed her my ladybugs.

"I can do better than *tell* you about ladybugs, Wanda," said the Friz. "I can *show* you!"

All of a sudden, Ms. Frizzle got "the look" — the one that tells us she has a far-out field trip in mind for us. We all knew what was coming next.

"To the bus, everyone!" she said. "A trip

to the park is just what we need to get intimate with insects."

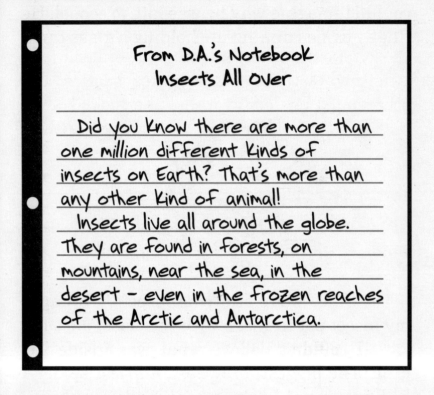

From D.A.'s Notebook
Insects All Over

Did you know there are more than one million different kinds of insects on Earth? That's more than any other kind of animal!

Insects live all around the globe. They are found in forests, on mountains, near the sea, in the desert — even in the frozen reaches of the Arctic and Antarctica.

"All right!" I exclaimed.

I put my ladybugs' box in my backpack, leaving the zipper partly open so Spot and Whirly would have enough air. Then I headed for the bus with everyone else.

It wasn't until we were all buckled in that we realized Ralphie was missing. I couldn't imagine why he was late to school. He finally came running up, holding a glass tank.

"Since we're studying insects, I brought my insect pet to share with the class," he said.

I couldn't believe what was inside the tank. The biggest, brownest, *hairiest* spider I had ever seen! Looking at it made me shiver. But Ralphie acted as if that creepy crawler was as cuddly as a teddy bear.

"This is Fang, my tarantula," he said proudly. "I just got him at the Paw & Claw pet shop."

It's a Tarantula!
by Ralphie

A tarantula has hairy legs, eight eyes, and a hairy body that's tan, reddish-brown, dark brown, or black. Tarantulas are the longest-living spiders on the planet. Some live to be more than twenty years old! They're big, too. An adult tarantula can have a leg span of more than 10 inches (25 cm). Tarantulas live in warm areas all around the world.

"Um, Ralphie? Spiders *aren't* insects, you know," said D.A.

Ralphie sure looked surprised to hear that. To tell you the truth, so was I.

"They're not?" I said.

D.A. took a book about insects from her backpack. "Spiders are arachnids. They're relatives of insects," she explained, "but they're a totally different kind of arthropod."

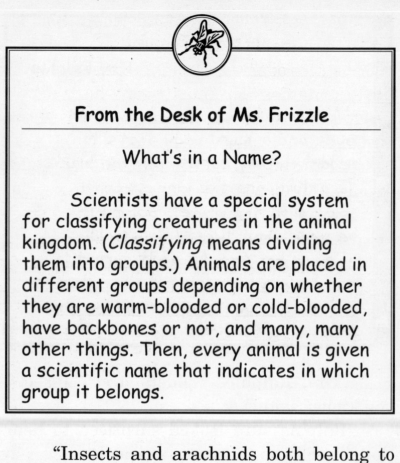

From the Desk of Ms. Frizzle

What's in a Name?

Scientists have a special system for classifying creatures in the animal kingdom. (*Classifying* means dividing them into groups.) Animals are placed in different groups depending on whether they are warm-blooded or cold-blooded, have backbones or not, and many, many other things. Then, every animal is given a scientific name that indicates in which group it belongs.

"Insects and arachnids both belong to a group of animals called *arthropods*," said Ms. Frizzle. "All arthropods have exoskeletons."

"Exo-*whats*?" Ralphie asked.

"Exoskeletons," the Friz said again.

"Skeletons they wear outside their bodies rather than inside."

Arthropods? Arachnids? Exoskeletons? All those names were making my head ache! "I just want to know what to feed my ladybugs," I said.

"And you will, Wanda!" Ms. Frizzle promised. "But getting acquainted with insects is an important first step, don't you think?"

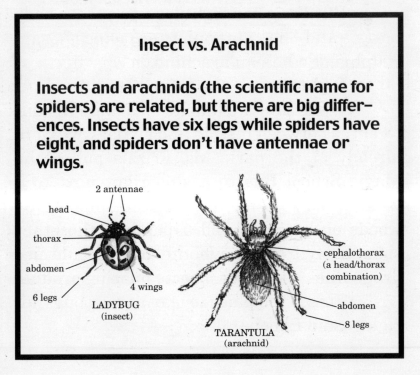

Insect vs. Arachnid

Insects and arachnids (the scientific name for spiders) are related, but there are big differences. Insects have six legs while spiders have eight, and spiders don't have antennae or wings.

2 antennae

head

thorax

abdomen

6 legs

4 wings

LADYBUG
(insect)

cephalothorax
(a head/thorax
combination)

abdomen

8 legs

TARANTULA
(arachnid)

She took a poster from the glove compartment. While Ms. Frizzle drove, Liz held up the poster for us to see.

"So," said Keesha, "if you have an arthropod with three main body parts, six legs, and antennae, it's an insect!"

"Like Spot and Whirly," I added.

"You've got it!" said Ms. Frizzle. "Ladybugs belong to a group of insects called beetles."

"But Fang has eight legs, two main body parts, and no antennae or wings," said Ralphie. "So he's an arachnid."

"Right again!" Ms. Frizzle confirmed.

By the time we finished learning the differences between insects and spiders, we were already at the park. Ms. Frizzle pulled the Magic School Bus to a stop right next to a wide grassy lawn. It was surrounded by woods on one side and a pond on the other side. Even from inside the bus I could see dragonflies and other insects buzzing around.

"This is the place to learn about bugs, all right!" said Phoebe.

Everyone piled out. I held my backpack in my arms so I could keep an eye on Spot and Whirly. That must be why I didn't notice Ralphie getting off the bus at the same time I did.

Wham!

We crashed into each other and tumbled off the bus. My backpack went flying. So did Fang's tank. Ralphie's baseball cap shot through the air. Everything landed in a big heap on the grass — including Ralphie and me.

It took me a moment to realize that Spot and Whirly's box had fallen out of my backpack — and that the screen had popped off.

"My ladybugs are gone!" I cried. But when I thought about it, I wasn't too upset. "Maybe they need to be back in nature."

"What about Fang?" asked Carlos. "Does *he* need to be in nature, too?"

I saw that Fang's glass tank was on its side. Pebbles from the bottom spilled out onto the grass. So did Fang!

"Catch him!" Leaving his hat in the grass, Ralphie scrambled after the tarantula. But it was too late.

Fang scuttled into the tall grass on his eight long legs. In an instant, he was gone from sight.

"This is bad," Ralphie said, frowning. "Tarantulas are used to warm weather. It could get cold soon. And what will he eat?"

Home Is Where the Habitat Is
by Carlos

The environment an animal needs to live and grow in is called its habitat. Before adopting a pet, it's important to make sure you can give it the food and home that are right for it.

"What does Fang *usually* eat?" asked Keesha.

"All spiders are predators," Ralphie told us. "They hunt other animals for food."

Predators and Prey
by Wanda

A predator is an animal that lives by hunting other animals. An animal that is hunted by a predator for food is called its prey.

I didn't like the sound of that. Not one bit. "What kinds of animals?" I asked.

"Insects, mostly," said Ralphie. "Crickets, grasshoppers, beetles . . ."

I gasped. "Ms. Frizzle, didn't you just tell me ladybugs are a kind of beetle?" I said. "What if Spot and Whirly become Fang's lunch?"

14

CHAPTER 2

All of a sudden, leaving my ladybugs in nature didn't seem like such a good idea. I had to do something — *anything* — to make sure Spot and Whirly didn't turn into spider food.

"Don't worry, Wanda. Fang just ate a cricket this morning. He's probably not even hungry," Ralphie told me. He looked around with worried eyes. "My dad warned me not to bring Fang. What if he bites someone? What if he's lost forever?"

"We need to find Fang *and* the lady-bugs," D.A. said. "Then we'll know *everyone's* okay."

Good News and Bad News about Tarantulas

by D.A.

The bad news is that a tarantula's bite is venomous. That means it contains venom, a kind of poison.

The good news is that tarantulas don't bite often. A tarantula bite isn't very harmful to humans. There might be a little swelling, numbness, and itching, but those symptoms usually disappear quickly. To be safe, always wash a tarantula bite to keep it from getting infected.

D.A. always has big ideas. How were we supposed to find two tiny ladybugs and a spider in that humongous park?

I should have known the Friz would have a plan. "Not to worry," she told us. "It's like I always say, the best way to *find* a beetle is to *be* a beetle. Back on the bus, everyone!"

Beetle Mania

by Tim

Beetles are the largest group of insects. There are 500,000 different kinds! One out of every four animals on the planet is a beetle. So wherever you are, chances are there's a beetle close by.

Ralphie and I were in such a hurry to find our pets that we didn't bother to pick up our backpacks. Ralphie even left his baseball cap in the grass. As soon as we were all on board, the Friz pushed a button on the dashboard. The Magic School Bus shrank down to the size of a bug. And that was just the beginning!

"Hey! The bus is sprouting legs," said Tim.

D.A. looked out the window. "Six of them!" she said. "Not to mention three main body parts and two antennae. We're an insect!"

"Not just any insect. We're a tiger beetle. See our special hardware?" said Ms. Frizzle. She moved a lever, and a pair of hard, shiny green wings curved out from the top of the bus.

Beetles Are Tough
by Phoebe

The main thing that makes beetles different from other insects is their elytra – their hard front wings. Elytra are like armor that protects a second pair of wings and the beetle's soft abdomen.

"All beetles have four wings," the Friz told us. "Their elytra are for protection. They use their more flexible wings to fly."

I was happy to know Spot and Whirly had their polka-dot pattern to protect them — wherever they were. If only I knew how to find them!

Hide-and-seek
by Keesha

Many beetles have brightly colored elytra with bold markings on them. The special markings help to distract predators so they can't see the whole beetle. That makes it easier for beetles to blend in with their surroundings.

Ms. Frizzle seemed to read my mind. "Now, all we have to do to find your pets is find their food."

"You mean, if we can find the kind of food ladybugs and spiders eat, we'll find Spot, Whirly, and Fang?" asked Carlos.

Ms. Frizzle grinned. "Absolutely. So let's get dirty! Take chances! It's time to find our bugs!"

Then the Friz pressed another button, and the bus darted off toward the woods. It zigzagged back and forth over the grass, just like a tiger beetle.

Tiger Beetles Get Around
by Carlos

Tiger beetles live everywhere in the world except the Antarctic and Tasmania. They have long jawbones, long legs, big eyes, and a wide head. All beetles are colorful, too. Their elytra are usually bright and have bold markings.

All tiger beetles are predators. They have powerful jaws, called mandibles, that they use to hold and crush their prey.

Let me tell you, things looked really different from a beetle's point of view. Every blade of grass was as tall as a tree. Clods of dirt were like huge boulders. And the actual trees were *gigantic*!

"Beetles at four o'clock!" called Tim as Ms. Frizzle steered the Magic Beetle Bus between the trees.

Dozens of shiny green tiger beetles scuttled around in a clearing. They weren't alone, either. Not by a long shot! Lots of ants, caterpillars, spiders, and other bugs crawled nearby on the leaves, dirt, and branches. I wasn't sure I liked being around crawling creatures that were just as big as we were. But I had to find Spot and Whirly.

"Okay, we found some tiger beetles. But where's their food?" I wondered.

Just then, a tiger beetle ran right in front of us, chasing a brown-striped spider.

"Does that answer your question?" asked D.A.

Ralphie frowned. "I hope Fang stays away from tiger beetles," he said.

D.A. showed us a page in her insect book. "It says here that tiger beetles are predators, like spiders," she said. "They hunt other insects and arthropods for food."

"Other insects?" I repeated. "Like lady-bugs?"

"Insects *do* have a tendency to eat one another," said Ms. Frizzle.

"It's a bug-eat-bug world out here," said Carlos.

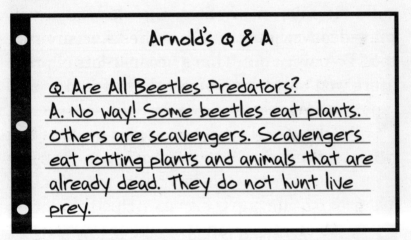

Arnold's Q & A

Q. Are All Beetles Predators?
A. No way! Some beetles eat plants. Others are scavengers. Scavengers eat rotting plants and animals that are already dead. They do not hunt live prey.

"Ugh!" Arnold covered his ears with his hands. "That's more than I want to know!"

"But," the Friz went on, "ladybugs have ways of defending themselves against predators. Even against other beetles."

I sure was glad to hear that!

"According to my research, ladybugs and other beetles give off a bad smell that helps keep predators away," D.A. said.

Phoebe crinkled up her nose. "I never thought making a stink could be a *good* thing," she said. "But I guess it is if it keeps predators from eating you."

"It says in my book that ladybugs will play dead when there's a predator around, too," D.A. went on. "That's because lots of predators won't attack an insect that isn't moving."

Ladybugs Carry Warning Labels
by Wanda

The red-and-black or yellow-and-black coloring of ladybugs is like a warning sign to birds. Most insects with that type of coloring don't taste good, so birds learn to leave them alone. That's good news for ladybugs!

All of a sudden, I saw something that *was* moving. Something red and black that flew up out of some wildflowers at the edge of the clearing.

"It's Spot and Whirly!" I said.

"Aha!" Ms. Frizzle steered the bus across the ground toward the flowers.

That was when we noticed the ants. Red ants. Way more than I could *ever* count! They looked like a red carpet that swarmed over the ground.

"Oh, no!" breathed Keesha.

But Ms. Frizzle looked as if we had just hit the insect jackpot.

"Those ants are doing exactly what they should be," she said. "Hunting for food."

"No wonder Spot and Whirly flew out of here," Tim said. "They don't want to be eaten!"

Arnold's face turned a pale, greenish color. "Neither do I!" he said.

The ants looked like an army of scary, six-legged aliens, but that wasn't the worst part.

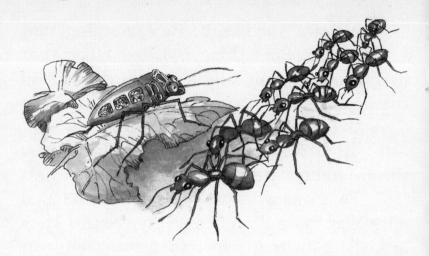

The worst part was that every single
one of those creatures was marching straight
toward us.

CHAPTER 3

"Hold on to your seats," said the Friz. "We're going to buzz out of here!"

She pushed the lever on the dashboard, and the two hard elytra on top of the bus spread out. The Magic Beetle Bus leaped into the air and used its second pair of wings to fly out of reach of the ants.

"The teachers at my old school never told us to buzz off," said Phoebe.

"I'm just glad we're safe." D.A. breathed a sigh of relief. "Having wings is definitely handy for getting away from predators on the prowl."

"*And* for chasing down lost ladybugs," I said.

"And Fang!" Ralphie reminded us.

As the Magic Beetle Bus buzzed through the air, we all looked out the windows.

"Uh-oh," Carlos said, pointing back to where the ants swarmed over the ground. "I don't see any ladybugs or Fang, but look at that caterpillar! There's no way it can get away from the ants."

Down on the ground, a green caterpillar tried to wriggle away. But it just couldn't get up enough speed. The ants were all over it in a second!

"What's happening?" Tim asked.

"The ants are stinging the caterpillar. Their sting contains venom," Ms. Frizzle told us. "When several of the ants have stung the caterpillar, the poison is strong enough to kill it. That's how ants kill prey that's so much bigger than they are."

I felt bad about leaving the poor caterpillar. But we had a mission. "I can't believe Spot and Whirly disappeared again!" I said. "We've got to find them and Fang."

Using our elytra and flying wings, the

Magic Beetle Bus flew from branch to branch. I'd bet we searched every bush and flower in the woods. But did we find our pets? No such luck.

Heavy Artillery

by Tim

The venom of some ants is so strong that it can make a person faint.

"Look!" Tim pointed toward the ground below a tree branch, where Ms. Frizzle landed the Magic Beetle Bus. "Aren't those the ants we saw before?" he asked.

It was the red ants, all right. They still had the caterpillar. That huge creepy-crawler seemed way too big to carry. But the ants had moved it out of the woods. They managed to lift and drag it by using their mandibles.

"Why didn't the ants just eat the caterpillar where they found it?" Ralphie asked.

"Carrying that gigantic thing looks like a lot of work."

"That caterpillar will be food for *all* the ants in the colony," Ms. Frizzle said. "When ants catch prey, they take it back to their nest for everyone to share."

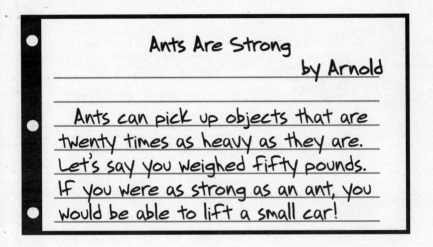

Ants Are Strong
by Arnold

Ants can pick up objects that are twenty times as heavy as they are. Let's say you weighed fifty pounds. If you were as strong as an ant, you would be able to lift a small car!

"I get it. Ants work together to make sure the entire colony grows and stays healthy," Carlos said.

"Right you are, Carlos. Ants are some of the best team players in the insect world," said the Friz. "They're small. But when they join forces, they do *big* work."

From the Desk of Ms. Frizzle

Ants Live and Work Together

Ants are social insects that live in groups called *colonies*. Different ants have special jobs:

- A *queen's* job is to mate and lay eggs. There is usually just one queen in each colony.
- *Males* have one job: to mate with queen ants.
- *Workers* are females who can't reproduce. They do the rest of the work in the colony. They hunt, protect and fix the anthill, care for hatching eggs, and feed the queen and growing ants.

"Ants can do big work—like killing that caterpillar for food," said Tim.

Down below us, the ants carried the caterpillar toward a big mound of sticks and leaves and dirt heaped against the side of an old tree stump.

"Is that their nest?" Arnold asked.

Ms. Frizzle gave a contented nod. "Inside that anthill, thousands of ants are hard at work taking care of ant eggs. Hatching eggs need lots of food to grow and change into adult ants."

Home Sweet Home
by Phoebe

Many ants live in nests called anthills. Ants use twigs, leaves, and dirt to make a hill above the ground. They burrow into the hill and beneath the ground, making lots and lots of tunnels and chambers.

From the Desk of Ms. Frizzle

Big Changes for Bugs

All insects hatch from eggs. Most insect babies are called *larvae*, and they look very different from adult insects. Larvae go through many stages before becoming adults. This process is called *metamorphosis*. Here's how it works:

- A larva hatches from an egg. As it grows, the larva sheds its skin. This is called *molting*.
- After molting a few times, the larva becomes a *pupa*. During the pupa stage, the larva changes to an adult insect, with six legs, two antennae, and three body parts.
- After that, the adult insect doesn't molt anymore. Its metamorphosis is complete!

I had no idea insects went through so many changes! "I just hope Spot and Whirly don't change into bug food," I said.

Ms. Frizzle hit the gas, and the Magic Beetle Bus flew off again. But instead of seeing my ladybugs or Ralphie's tarantula, we saw a bunch of really tiny insects. There were hundreds of them swarming all over some nearby flower stems.

"Those bugs you see are aphids," explained Ms. Frizzle. "They are sucking sap from the flower stems for food."

Hungry, Hungry Aphids
by D.A.

Aphids are very small, but they feed in big groups and can cause large amounts of damage to plants. There are many different kinds of aphids and they feed on all types of plants – including flowers, vegetables, and fruit trees.

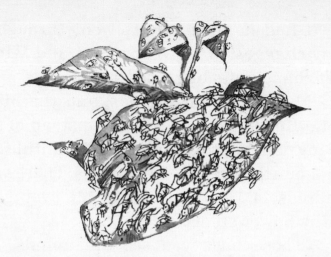

"It's nice to see some insects still eat plants, instead of eating other bugs," Keesha said as she looked out the window.

"Actually, Keesha," the Friz began, "aphids cause a lot of problems for gardeners and farmers. Their eating habits can kill plants and trees."

I could tell that we could spend the whole day learning about insects, but I was more interested in *finding* insects. My lady-bugs were still missing in action! I was just about to remind Ms. Frizzle about our pets when she started talking to herself.

"Hmm. If we're going to find Fang and

the ladybugs, I think we need more eye power," Ms. Frizzle said.

When I saw the sparkle in her eyes, I knew the Friz had something special in mind. Boy, was I right!

"Class," she said, "it's time for a little metamorphosis!"

CHAPTER 4

"Something tells me things are about to change — in a big way!" said Keesha.

Ms. Frizzle pushed a button, and the Magic Beetle Bus turned back into the Magic School Bus.

"The bus isn't the only thing that's changing," said Arnold. "We are, too!"

He was right. We were changing. And how! We sprouted antennae, two pairs of long, shimmering blue-green wings, six legs, three main body parts, and two large, bulging eyes.

"We're dragonflies!" I said.

"Now *that's* metamorphosis!" said Carlos.

Using her four wings, Ms. Frizzle flew

out the Magic School Bus door. "Dragonflies have some of the best eye power in the insect world," she said. "When it comes to spotting other insects, they can't be beat. So let's go!"

Seeing Is Believing
by Carlos

Most of a dragonfly's head is taken up by its two compound eyes — eyes that are made up of many smaller eyes. Each compound eye is made of twenty to twenty-five thousand tiny eyes. That's a lot of seeing power! Compound eyes are especially good at seeing moving things — such as flying insects.

We left Liz at the wheel of the Magic School Bus, and followed Ms. Frizzle. Our wings hummed as we flew through the air. I looked out through my new compound eyes. We all had on special goggles that would help us see like dragonflies. Talk about amazing!

"With all these eyes on the job," said D.A., "we'll find Spot, Whirly, and Fang in no time!"

She wasn't kidding, either. As soon as I flew out of the trees and into the bright sunshine, I spotted my ladybugs!

"They're flying toward the pond," I said. "Come on!"

We flew after them. At least, Arnold, D.A., Carlos, Ms. Frizzle, and I did. Everyone else stayed behind to look for Fang.

"We want to save you!" I called out.

But did they listen? No way! Spot and Whirly flew away from us faster than ever. Before we could catch up, they disappeared into the tall grass at the edge of the pond.

"I'm afraid Spot and Whirly see us as predators," Ms. Frizzle told us. "That's why they've gone into hiding."

"After all, a predator has to *find* a bug before it can *eat* it," said Carlos.

If my ladybugs were trying to protect themselves by keeping still and blending in with their surroundings, they were doing a great job. Too great. How were we ever going to find them?

"Why would Spot and Whirly think we want to eat them?" Arnold asked.

"Dragonflies are fantastic hunters," D.A. answered. "And fast." Just as she said that, a dragonfly whizzed by us.

Faster Than a Speeding Dragonfly
by Wanda

Dragonflies can fly forward and backward. They change paths so quickly that they're hard to follow. Dragonflies are fast, too. They can reach speeds of thirty miles per hour — faster than most kids can ride a bike down a hill.

"Ugh!" Arnold winced as the dragonfly caught a mosquito in midair.

"Isn't it marvelous to see the food chain in action?" Ms. Frizzle said, beaming. "A hunting dragonfly is truly a wonder to behold. See how it uses its front legs and powerful mandibles to hold that mosquito?"

I couldn't bear to watch any more. "Guys, we've got to find my ladybugs . . . before a dragonfly does!"

We flew toward the long grass at the edge of the pond. More dragonflies rested on the long green blades with their four wings spread out wide.

That was *not* what I wanted to see. Not at all! "Spot and Whirly will never come out of hiding with all these hunters around," I said.

"Don't forget," said Ms. Frizzle. "In the insect world, even the mightiest hunters can be *hunted,* too."

We were really surprised to hear that.

"Even a dragonfly?" said Carlos. He tried some fancy moves with his dragonfly wings, zipping left and right so fast it made me dizzy. "What kind of insect could be big enough, fast enough, and have enough eye power to catch *us*?"

French-Fried Dragonflies?
                              by Arnold

Did you know that in some parts of the world, dragonflies are considered a delicacy? They are eaten fried with onions.

Arnold glanced behind us with his compound goggles. "What about a fly?" he said. "A huge gray one with spiny legs, black markings, and a bearded face."

"That sounds like a kind of robber fly," said the Friz. "They *do* eat dragonflies, as a matter of fact."

Arnold gulped. "I was afraid of that," he said. "Don't look now, but there's one right behind us."

CHAPTER 5

Learning about insects was turning out to be more than I bargained for. A lot more. Hungry ants, killer dragonflies, and now this!

I couldn't resist peeking behind us at the robber fly. As soon as I did, I wished I hadn't. That fly was huge! And it was headed our way.

"Quick! Come in for a landing, everyone," Ms. Frizzle instructed, pointing toward a grassy patch at the edge of the pond.

She didn't have to tell us to be quick. With that robber fly zooming up, we didn't

waste a second. Flapping our dragonfly wings at top speed, we streaked toward a long blade of grass.

"It's lucky for us dragonflies are so fast," I said.

Even though we were fast, the robber fly stayed on our trail — until we landed on the grass.

"Phew! He's flying away," said Arnold, resting on the long grass with his four wings spread out to the side.

"Robber flies and dragonflies both prefer to catch their prey in midair," Ms. Frizzle said. "It's harder for them to see insects that aren't moving, so they lose interest in them."

Robber Flies Are Good Hunters
by Carlos

Robber flies are fast predators that hunt flying insects such as wasps, bees, and dragonflies. They even hunt prey that is larger than they are.

Carlos looked at the rest of us. "That's the first time I was *glad* another creature thought I was boring," he said.

"According to my research, robber flies have a secret weapon that helps them hunt," D. A. said, watching the robber fly buzz through the air. "See that sharp mouth part?"

How could we miss it! It looked like a pointy beak sticking out of the fly's hairy face.

"Robber flies use their beak to stab prey," Ms. Frizzle explained.

Bug Soup

by Keesha

Robber flies inject their prey with saliva and digestive juices. This paralyzes the prey and turns its insides to liquid, which the robber fly then sucks up.

"Eeew!" said Arnold. "No wonder my mom says flies are pests."

"Fly predators aren't all bad," Ms. Frizzle pointed out. "Some, like hover flies, eat bugs that kill garden plants."

"Like the aphids we saw drinking sap from the wildflowers?" I asked.

Ms. Frizzle nodded. "Exactly! If insect predators didn't eat aphids and other garden pests, a lot *more* plants would be destroyed."

"I never thought of flies as friends before," said Carlos. "I guess even insect predators can do good deeds."

Just then, the robber fly zoomed after a bumblebee. Yuck. I could imagine what would happen next. "Let's get out of here," I said.

We flew away from the pond, searching for Spot and Whirly among the grass and shrubs and trees. We didn't see them anywhere! But we *did* see Ralphie, Keesha, Tim, and Phoebe. They were just flying in for a landing on the branches of a flowering azalea bush.

"Any sign of Fang?" Carlos asked.

Are All Flies Predators?
by Arnold

No way! Many flies, like mosquitoes, are parasites. They sting larger animals and drink their blood for food, but they don't kill them.

Other flies, like houseflies, are scavengers. They eat food that they find, including animals that are already dead, old plants, leftovers, even animal dung. Because they eat things that carry germs, scavengers often spread disease.

Ralphie shook his head. He looked really worried. We all were.

"Just remember, Ralphie," said the Friz, flapping her four dragonfly wings. "If at first you don't succeed, fly, fly again!"

That sounded like good advice to me. I

was ready to take off and keep searching. Until I heard D.A. shriek, that is.

"Stay still!" Keesha said. "There's *another* insect predator."

That was the last thing I wanted to hear. I looked all around, but I didn't see anything but branches, leaves, and flowers.

"Over there." Keesha pointed to a green branch on our left.

At least it *looked* like a branch. Then I

saw a long body, six sticklike legs, a triangle-shaped head with two bulging compound eyes, and antennae. All those body parts belonged to an insect, all right. One that stood so very, very still that it looked just like part of the bush.

"Wow," I said. "A praying mantis."

CHAPTER 6

That praying mantis was so cool-looking! For a minute, we all just stayed on the azalea bush and watched it.

"Praying mantises are amazing masters of disguise," Ms. Frizzle told us. "Their shape and coloring make it easy for them to blend into the background. They can stay perfectly still for a very long time. Other animals don't even know they're there."

"Until it's too late," said Carlos.

Arnold shivered. "Please tell me that praying mantis isn't hunting us," he said.

"According to my research, praying mantises don't usually chase their prey, like dragon-flies and ants," said D.A. "They stay in one place and wait for passing insects, then attack them."

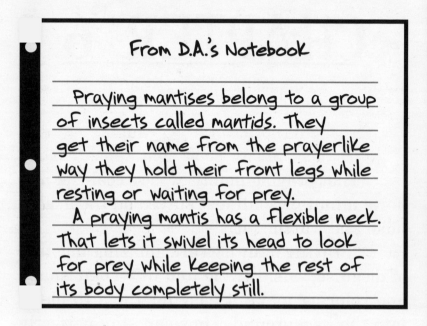

From D.A.'s Notebook

Praying mantises belong to a group of insects called mantids. They get their name from the prayerlike way they hold their front legs while resting or waiting for prey.

A praying mantis has a flexible neck. That lets it swivel its head to look for prey while keeping the rest of its body completely still.

"Quite right, D.A.!" said the Friz. "But just to be on the safe side, I'm going to call our safe ride."

With that said, Ms. Frizzle let out a loud whistle. A moment later, the Magic School Bus headed our way with Liz at the wheel.

Was I ever glad to get back on that bus. Not only did we turn back into kids, but we could watch the praying mantis from behind the safety of windows.

"I know we're in the bus, but let's keep our distance from that praying mantis," Ralphie said. He looked through the bus windows at the sharp spines on the mantid's front legs. "I do *not* want to get caught in those."

"It says in my book that those grabby legs are another reason mantids are such great hunters," D.A. told us. "Mantids snatch and hold prey with their front legs. Next they chew on their prey to make it stop moving, and then they eat it alive."

"Gross!" said Phoebe.

"Insect predators may seem ruthless to us," said the Friz, "but don't forget, every living creature needs food. By eating other bugs, insect predators help to keep the balance between *all* creatures on Earth."

"Praying mantises seem like the kings of the insect predator world, but they still have to protect themselves against other hunters, right?" said Carlos.

"Like birds," said Keesha, watching a cardinal fly overhead.

Ms. Frizzle nodded. "And bats. But mantids have their ways of staying safe. They know how to keep still, and they're very good listeners."

Mantids Have Manners!
by Phoebe

When a mantid is done eating, it will wipe its face clean!

Mantids are picky eaters, too. If any part of their prey is dropped, they won't eat it.

The mantid on our bush hadn't moved a mandible the whole time we watched it. But all of a sudden I saw something *else* move. Two red ladybugs with black spots.

"Spot and Whirly!" I said.

Ralphie scratched his head, looking around. "I still haven't seen Fang *anywhere*," he said.

I was really worried about Fang, too. But was I ever glad to see my ladybugs! They buzzed through the air toward our flowering azalea bush.

"Uh-oh." Tim bit his lip, watching the praying mantis. "We're not the only ones who see Spot and Whirly."

The mantid's compound eyes followed my ladybugs through the air.

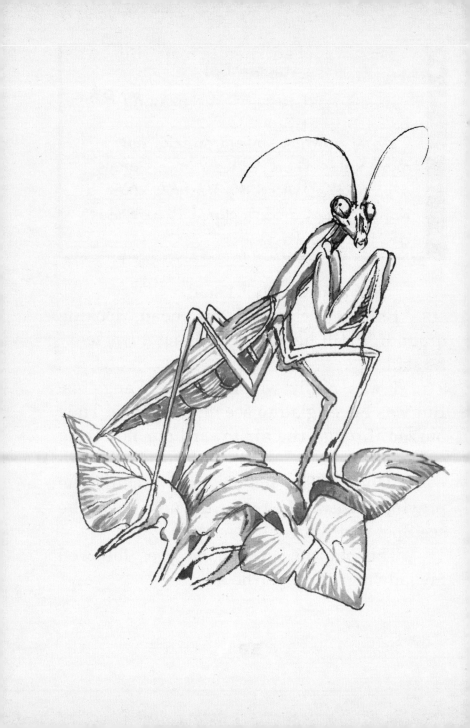

This was bad. Really bad. But what could we do?

In the next instant, the praying mantis moved with lightning speed.

Faster Than the Eye Can See
by Tim

A mantid's strike takes just thirty to fifty one-thousandths of a second. That's too fast to be processed by the human brain.

CHAPTER 7

"I can't look!" said Phoebe.

Believe me, I wasn't crazy about the idea of watching my ladybugs get crunched in the mantid's spiny legs, either. Spot and Whirly didn't deserve to turn into another insect's lunch!

But you know what? We had been so busy watching the praying mantis, we didn't notice a spiderweb right next to it. The web was like a sticky net that filled the space between branches of the azalea bush. When I finally *did* look, I saw that the praying mantis was caught right smack in the middle of the web. And when I looked back to where Spot and Whirly had been, I saw them flying away.

"Great! My ladybugs are safe — for now," I said.

"The praying mantis sure isn't," Tim pointed out. "Look at that spider!"

A brown spider crawled out from the edge of the web. It rushed across the lines of the web toward the praying mantis.

Why Don't Spiders Get Stuck?
by Keesha

Spiders know their own webs. They know to keep away from the sticky threads of silk and walk only on the dry ones.

Spiders often coat their legs with a kind of oil from their mouths, too. The oil helps to keep their feet from getting caught in case they do happen to step on a sticky thread.

"Right on schedule!" said the Friz. "When the praying mantis hit the web, it made the web vibrate. That sent a signal to the orb spider."

"So *that's* how it knows its next meal is ready," said Keesha.

I couldn't believe how fast the orb spider moved across the dry strands of silk. The mantid struggled, but it couldn't get free of the sticky web. When the spider reached it, it bit right into the mantid's neck with its fangs.

"Yikes!" said Carlos. "The mighty mantid is going to end up *being* a snack instead of *having* one."

"The spider used its fangs to inject venom into the mantid," Ms. Frizzle explained.

"You mean like that robber fly we saw?" I asked.

The Friz nodded. "Sometimes a spider's venom is strong enough to kill its prey immediately. Other times, the venom just paralyzes the prey."

Sure enough, the praying mantis stopped moving. The orb spider went right to work. It wrapped the mantid in sticky silk until it looked like an insect mummy.

Spider Silk Is Superstrong
by Arnold

Spider silk is one of the strongest materials on the planet — stronger even than the steel used to make high-rise buildings. A rope of spider silk one inch (2.5cm) thick could hold up fifty cars!

"Spiders don't eat their prey alive, like dragonflies and mantids," said Ms. Frizzle.

"That's right," Ralphie said. "Spiders are more like robber flies. Once a spider injects its prey with poison, all it has to do is suck up the liquid, and lunch is served!" Ralphie finished. "That's how Fang eats, anyway."

"Eeew!" said Arnold. He looked as if he might get sick.

I knew how he felt. We were all relieved when the orb spider left the mantid alone and went back to the edge of its web.

"I think we've learned enough. Can we get out of here now?" Arnold wanted to know.

Spiders Chow Down
by Carlos

If you could weigh all the insects that spiders eat in one year, it would weigh more than all the people on Earth!

Ms. Frizzle got behind the wheel of the Magic School Bus. I noticed that Ralphie was pretty quiet. He bit his lip, staring out the windows of the bus with worried eyes.

"Ms. Frizzle?" I said. "We haven't seen a

single sign of Fang. Isn't there something else we can do to find him?"

"There certainly is, Wanda!" said the Friz. "We've already gotten an insect's view of the park. Now it's time to see what an arachnid can see."

She pressed a button on the dashboard, and the bus grew eight long legs. Eight dark eyes sprouted above the front windshield. A

dark brown stripe ran down the center of the bus's two main body parts.

"I guess it *takes* a spider to *find* a spider," Tim said.

"My thoughts exactly!" said Ms. Frizzle.

As she steered the Magic Spider Bus down the bush toward the ground, Keesha gazed curiously at the orb spider's web.

"How come Fang's tank didn't have any spiderwebs in it, Ralphie?" she asked.

Ralphie's Hunting-Spider Facts

Hunting spiders depend on leg strength and speed to catch their prey, not on webs.

Some hunting spiders lie in wait for their prey, hiding on leaves or flowers. Others live in burrows. They hide inside and then dart out to catch passing prey.

Ralphie shrugged. "Not all spiders make webs," he said. "Fang catches prey by hunting for it, not by trapping it in a web."

Ms. Frizzle grinned from ear to ear. "Right you are, Ralphie!" she told him. "Hunting spiders are fast runners. They go out and search for prey. When they find food, they chase it down with a burst of spider speed."

Watch out for Black Widows?
by Wanda

Black widows are small, shiny black spiders with red hourglass markings. Their venom can be fifteen times more powerful than rattlesnake poison!

Black widow spiders often live close to people — in woodpiles, trash, and the lids of garbage cans. Black widows sometimes bite in self-defense. If you are bitten, you should see a doctor right away.

Arnold looked around nervously. "Do *all* spiders have fangs that inject venom?"

"Yes, but don't worry. Most spiders can't hurt humans," Ms. Frizzle assured him. "The ones that can, like tarantulas and black widows, only bite when they feel threatened or in danger. Even then, their bite is usually no worse than a bee sting."

"Spiders aren't all bad. They do a lot of good in the world," Ralphie said.

The Friz nodded. "You said it, Ralphie. Spiders eat tons of insect pests."

Spiders Help Out
by Carlos

Spiders eat flies that can carry disease, bees that sting, mosquitoes that bite, moth larvae that make holes in cloth, and insects that destroy crops. Without spiders, the world wouldn't be nearly as comfortable or safe.

"Spiders really *can* do good work — especially with eight hands on the job," Carlos said.

"And a sticky web." I looked out the window. High above us, the praying mantis was still all wrapped up in spider silk in the orb spider's web. "Thanks to that orb spider and its web, we can keep looking for our pets."

"Absolutely!" Ms. Frizzle steered the Magic Spider Bus off the azalea bush and onto the ground. "We're back on the insect trail!"

CHAPTER 8

We all kept our eyes peeled for Fang, Spot, and Whirly. We didn't see them right away. But we sure did *hear* something. A buzzing noise. And boy, was it loud!

"Is it engine trouble?" Tim wondered.

But it was something much worse. A wasp! It buzzed right over the Magic Spider Bus.

"Let me guess. Wasps are predators, too," I said.

"Not all wasps are predators, but that one is," said the Friz. "Isn't it great?"

"Red alert," said D.A. "According to my research, some wasps hunt spiders!"

Wasps' Ways

by D.A.

Wasps belong to the same insect group as ants and bees. They have thin waists that allow them to move their tail ends around. At the very tip of the tail end is the wasp's stinger – a sharp, tubelike spear that contains its venom sac.

Lots of wasps live in colonies, like ants, with queens, males, and female workers. But not all wasps are social. Some are solitary, which means they live alone in burrows and hunt and care for their young themselves.

For some reason, Ms. Frizzle didn't seem nearly as scared as the rest of us. "Spiders have their ways of keeping out of harm's way," she said.

She steered the bus toward some leaves on the ground. The Friz moved a lever on the dashboard, and the Magic Spider Bus used its front legs to lift the leaves.

"A trapdoor!" said Tim. "Cool!"

Beneath the door was a spider's burrow. The Magic Spider Bus scrambled in on its eight legs, and the trapdoor dropped back into place over the entrance.

"This burrow belongs to a trapdoor spider, class," explained Ms. Frizzle. "I'm sure it won't mind if we borrow its home for a few minutes."

Ms. Frizzle used the bus's legs to raise the trapdoor a crack so we could watch the wasp. Now that we were safe inside the burrow, the wasp couldn't get us. But we saw *another* spider that wasn't so lucky. A brown trapdoor spider scuttled toward another burrow — but not fast enough.

"Uh-oh," said Phoebe. She winced as the wasp stung the trapdoor spider right near its mouth.

"Ugh! I know the food chain is an impor-

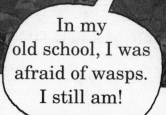

tant part of life on Earth," I said, squeezing my eyes shut, "but that doesn't mean I have to *watch* it!"

"Not to worry, Wanda," said Ms. Frizzle. "That trapdoor spider isn't going to become wasp food until later."

I opened my eyes again. "It isn't?"

"Nope," D.A. said. "Adult wasps mostly eat flower nectar, not other insects."

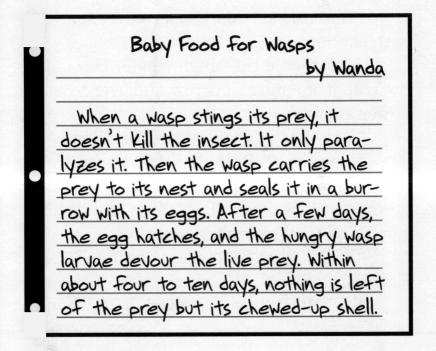

Baby Food for Wasps
by Wanda

When a wasp stings its prey, it doesn't kill the insect. It only paralyzes it. Then the wasp carries the prey to its nest and seals it in a burrow with its eggs. After a few days, the egg hatches, and the hungry wasp larvae devour the live prey. Within about four to ten days, nothing is left of the prey but its chewed-up shell.

"When they *do* hunt live prey," Ms. Frizzle said, "they take it to their nest and leave it as food for their hatching eggs."

I have to admit, I was learning a lot about insect predators. Way more than I ever wanted to know!

"I'm just glad my pet insects are cute little ladybugs and not wasps," I said. "Spot and Whirly would never hurt a fly — or any other insect!"

"Want to bet?" Ms. Frizzle's eyes sparkled with challenge.

She steered the Magic Spider Bus out of the trapdoor spider's burrow and over to some flower stems.

"Hey! Look up, everyone," said Tim.

"Is it Fang?" Ralphie asked hopefully.

Arnold shook his head. Fang was still nowhere to be seen. But Spot and Whirly were. And they weren't alone!

"Look, they're eating aphids!" said Keesha.

I wouldn't have believed it if I hadn't

seen it with my own eyes. But there were Spot and Whirly, greedily gobbling up aphid after tiny aphid.

"Oh, no!" I said. "My ladybugs *aren't* just cute little insects. They're fierce predators."

CHAPTER 9

"Ladybugs aren't criminals, Wanda," Ms. Frizzle pointed out. "Eating other creatures is what insect predators are *supposed* to do."

When I thought about it, I realized she was right. "I guess ladybugs have to eat *something*," I said. "By eating aphids, they help to get rid of pests that destroy lots of plants, trees, and flowers."

"That's a *good* thing for plants — and for the people who grow them," said Carlos.

"Right you are!" Ms. Frizzle agreed.

Now that we had found my ladybugs, we started to come up with a plan to catch them. But my heart just wasn't in it.

"Spot and Whirly are doing fine taking care of themselves in the wild," I said. "Maybe we should leave them there."

"They've done a great job of protecting themselves from predators," D.A. said. "And they've got plenty of food."

That was for sure. Spot and Whirly were eating up aphids as fast as they could find them!

"Anyway, there's no way I could ever find enough aphids to feed them," I said. "Taking them out of the wild would be a big mistake."

Ladybugs Are BIG Eaters
by Wanda

A single ladybug may eat more than 5,000 aphids in its lifetime. That's a lot of bug food!

I knew I had made the right decision. Spot and Whirly belonged right where they were.

"What about Fang?" asked Ralphie.

"He's used to a warm environment. It could start to get cold in a few weeks. We've got to find him."

I was beginning to imagine the worst. After all, we hadn't seen even the tiniest sign of Fang. What if a predator had gotten him!

Ms. Frizzle pressed a button, and the Magic Spider Bus began to scramble across the grass on its eight long legs. We kept our noses pressed against the windows and our eyes alert for Fang.

"Whoa!" I grabbed the seat in front of me as the ground trembled and shook. "What's going on?"

It felt like an earthquake. Except that this earthquake barked!

"It's a dog," said Phoebe.

We all watched as a huge golden retriever came loping across the grass in our direction. Trust me, when I say huge, I mean it. We were so small, that retriever looked like a galloping mountain range.

"My cousin's dog chases spiders," said Tim. "Maybe we should run for cover!"

Ms. Frizzle hit the gas, and the Magic
Spider Bus scuttled toward something that
looked like a huge red dome.

"My baseball cap!" cried Ralphie.

It lay in the grass right where Ralphie

had left it when we collided getting off the bus. Was I ever glad it was still there! We scuttled underneath it. A second later, the gigantic retriever thundered past.

"Big animals like dogs sure do shake things up for insects and arachnids," said Arnold.

So true! We all hung on to one another so we wouldn't fall down. It took a second before we saw that we weren't alone underneath Ralphie's cap.

"Is that . . . ?" Arnold said nervously.

"Fang!" cried Ralphie.

It was Ralphie's tarantula, all right. I never thought I would be happy to see a huge, hairy spider — especially one that was bigger than we were. But I was definitely happy to see Fang!

"I'd bet he's been hiding here this whole time," I said.

"Tarantulas have a fearsome reputation. But the truth is, they are very timid," Ms. Frizzle told us.

"Fang always runs to hide if anything

startles him," Ralphie added. "He was probably scared when Wanda and I fell out of the bus and he wanted some shelter."

D.A. nodded. "Tarantulas usually hide in burrows, like wolf spiders and trapdoor spiders," she said. "But your baseball cap was just as good, Ralphie."

Ms. Frizzle hit the gas. "Don't go anywhere, Fang. We'll be right back!" she called.

The Magic Spider Bus zoomed back out from beneath Ralphie's cap. We went faster and faster, until everything outside the bus windows was just a green blur.

The next thing we knew, the Magic Spider Bus was the Magic School Bus again. It was its regular size — and so were we! As soon as the Friz opened the door, Ralphie ran outside and picked up his cap.

"Yes!" Ralphie crowed. He scooped up Fang and held the tarantula gently in his palm. I picked up Fang's tank from the ground and took it over to Ralphie.

"Mission accomplished," said Carlos, grinning. "Fang is back where he belongs."

"And Spot and Whirly are back in nature where *they* belong," said Keesha.

Just then, my stomach growled so loudly that everyone on the bus heard it.

"Now all we have to do is put our lunch where *it* belongs," I said. "In our stomachs!"

Everyone cheered. I guess they were as starved as I was!

"How about a pit stop at Ben's Burgers?" suggested Ms. Frizzle.

We all looked at one another.

"No, thanks, Ms. Frizzle," I said. "After this field trip, I think we'll definitely want to go vegetarian."

Ms. Frizzle's Scrapbook of
Spider and Insect Stories

Did you ever think of spiders and insects as magical creatures? If you have, you're not the only one! People from lots of different cultures have told special stories about insects and spiders. Here are a few of them:

Arachnids get their name from an ancient Greek story about Arachne, a woman who wove cloth so perfectly that even the goddess Athena could not do better. After losing a weaving contest to Arachne, Athena became so jealous that she wanted Arachne killed. In the end, Athena turned Arachne into a spider instead, and Arachne spent the rest of her life spinning silk.

Native American tribes in Mexico tell the story of a spider god named Tocotl, who helped create the world by spinning a huge hammock to hold up the universe.

Ancient Egyptians believed scarab beetles were magical and holy. They carried scarab beetles as good-luck charms and wore jewelry decorated with scarab designs because they believed the beetle would protect them from danger.

In the 1800s, people in America believed that spiders could ward off disease. To keep healthy, they put a spider inside a nutshell and hung it around their neck.

In Polynesia, people say they can get to heaven by climbing a giant ladder of spider silk.

People in France once believed that if a child was lost, the praying mantis would point to show it the way home.

According to African legend, a mantid has the power to bring the dead back to life.

Join my class on all of our Magic School Bus adventures!

The Truth about Bats
The Search for the Missing Bones
The Wild Whale Watch
Space Explorers
Twister Trouble
The Giant Germ
The Great Shark Escape
Penguin Puzzle
Dinosaur Detectives
Expedition Down Under
Insect Invaders
Amazing Magnetism
Polar Bear Patrol
Electric Storm
Voyage to the Volcano
Butterfly Battle
Food Chain Frenzy